MANGO
The Long Haired
Ginger Cat

Grandma Krazy

Cover design and illustrations by Lauren Garcia

Hardback ISBN-13: 978-1-7342665-9-7
E-Book ISBN - 978-1-7342665-9-7
Paperback ISBN-13: 978-1-7342665-8-0

Library of Congress Control Number:
2020913903

The author would love your honest review on Amazon
https://www.amazon.com/s?k=grandma+krazy&ref=nb_sb_noss_1

Follow the author at
Grandmakrazy.com
http://www.grandmakrazy.com/
https://www.facebook.com/loveohana/
https://www.instagram.com/grandmakrazy/
https://twitter.com/grandmakrazy
YouTube - Storytime with Grandma Krazy

This book is dedicated to
the real Mango and all her cat sisters
who have tenderly comforted
the many foster children that
have come through our home.

May we all strive to be happy
with who we are and what we have.
—Grandma Krazy

Lauren Garcia
would like to dedicate her illustrations
To Diana and Arthur
Who unconditionally love her, and

For Bryan
Who gave her the most amazing
opportunity to live her dreams.

Mango watched the birds fly
through the sky every day.

"*If only I had wings to fly.
Then I would be a happy cat,*"
she thought.

Mango did not like being a
long haired ginger cat.

Her long hair was hard to take care of.

She was tired of her family rules
and did not want to do her chores.

She longed to fly free like the birds.

One day, Mango found a
beautiful sparkling rock.

She rubbed the dust off the rock.

The rock began to change colors.
First it was blue, then it was red.

Soon it was green,
then it turned purple.
A beautiful little cat fairy
suddenly appeared above the rock.

"Mango," she said,
"since you have found my special rock,
I will grant one wish
for each of the colors you see."

Mango could see blue, red,
green and purple. That meant
she had four wishes!

Mango instantly knew
her first wish. She chose
blue to start.

*"I wish for wings
so I can fly through the sky
like the birds!"*

Mango felt a tickle on her shoulders.
She was growing wings! She could fly
through the sky! Mango thought,
"I will be a happy cat
now that I have wings."

Mango flapped her wings and lifted off the ground. She flew straight home to show her family her beautiful new wings.

Mango could hardly wait to surprise her family. She burst through the door to show her mom. But Mom had never seen a cat with wings before!

"*Who are you?*" Mom asked.

"*It's me Mom! It's Mango!*"

Mom shook her head and replied,
"You are not our Mango.
Our Mango does not have wings.
Now run along home."

Mango was not a happy cat!

The wings could not make her happy
if her family did not recognize her.
Just then, Mango heard a lion roar.

"*That's it!*" she thought.

"*If I roar like a lion, I would be so loud my family would have to listen to me, then I could tell them who I am!*"

She would definitely be a happy cat
if she could roar like a lion
and fly like a bird.

"*For my red wish,*
I wish to roar like a lion."

Mango roared as she flew back
home to see her family.

Mango found her family
playing together outside.

Mango roared, *"Hello family!"*
Everyone looked up, terrified.
Mom rounded up the other cats,
sprinted inside, and bolted
the door shut.

Mango roared at the door, but
her mom would not let her in.

Mango begged and roared,
*"Mom! It's me, Mango!
Please let me inside!"*

Mom hissed,
"Stop roaring at me,
you strange creature!"

"You are not our Mango.
Our Mango does not have wings or
roar like a lion. Now run along home!!"

Mango was a very sad cat.
Her family didn't recognize
her anymore.

She scared her family so much
they had run away from her.

Mango wondered where she
would sleep for the night.

Mango noticed a beaver paddling through the river, building a house with its long, flat tail.

"That's it," Mango thought. "I will use my green wish to change my tail into a beaver tail. Then I could build a house to sleep in tonight."

Mango's tail felt funny as it turned into a beaver tail.

She tried to swish it around, but it was too heavy.

Mango jumped into the stream and started paddling with her tail.

Her wings got in the way sometimes.

She enjoyed the cool swim with her new flat tail.

She was careful not to roar and scare anyone.

It was hard work building
a house. Mango was tired.

Her eyes felt heavy and
her tummy grumbled.

She missed her family.

Mango was not a happy cat at all!

She remembered her mother's warm hug.

She thought about playing with her sisters.

She wanted her daddy to tuck her into bed.

Mango realized she had a
lot to be happy about.

She did not need wings, or a lion's
roar, or a beaver's tail to be happy.

She needed her family and she
needed to be herself: A simple, long
haired ginger cat named Mango!

Just then, Mango heard
the cat fairy say,
"*Mango, you have one wish left.*

*Are you ready to
make your purple wish?*"

Mango knew what her
last wish would be.

"Yes, I am ready,"
Mango said.
"For my purple wish, I wish
to be myself again."

With a big smile, the fairy said,
"That is an awesome wish,
that I will happily grant."

Just like that,
Mango was herself again!

Mango washed her long ginger
hair until it shined.

She decided her chores were
not so hard after all.

She would even do stinky chores like
cleaning the twins' litter boxes.

Mango scampered home as
fast as she could go.

When Mom saw Mango coming
she meowed,
"Now that is our Mango."

Her family greeted her
with hugs and kisses.

*"We were worried
sick about you, Mango!"*
Mom cried.

"We are really happy you are home,"
her sisters said.

Mango told her family about
the sparkly rock, the cat fairy,
and her four wishes.

Mom said,
*"Mango, we love you
just the way you are."*

"I know, Mama," said Mango.
"I did not like trying to be
something I am not.
From now on,
I am going to be
the best ME I can be!"

Mom purred as she licked Mango's ears to welcome her home.

Mango is a
VERY HAPPY
long haired ginger cat.

Name the things that you
have to be happy about.

....

....

....

....

....

....

....

....

What can you do to be the best you, you can be?

....

....

....

....

....

....

....

Made in the USA
Middletown, DE
15 February 2022

61189203R00042